TEDD ARNOLD

HUGGLY'S® HALLOWEEN

SCHOLASTIC INC. Cartwheel ·B·O·O·K·S·®

New York Toronto London Auckland Sydney
Mexico City New Delhi Hong Kong Buenos Aires

To Edie and Steve
— T. A.

Copyright © 2002 by Tedd Arnold.
All rights reserved. Published by Scholastic Inc.
HUGGLY and THE MONSTER UNDER THE BED are trademarks and/or registered trademarks of Tedd Arnold.
SCHOLASTIC, CARTWHEEL BOOKS, and associated logos are trademarks and/or registered trademarks of Scholastic Inc.

0-439-32449-1

Library of Congress Cataloging-in-Publication Data available.

12 11 10 9 8 7 6 5 4   02 03 04 05 06

Printed in the U.S.A.   24
First printing, September 2002

Huggly rushed into the Secret Slime Pit.

"Booter, Grubble, come quick!" he cried. "The people world is going crazy!"

"Let's have a look," said Booter.

"This I gotta see!" said Grubble.

They followed Huggly to a hatchway in the tunnel.

The hatchway opened underneath a bed in the people child's room where Huggly played.

"The people have all turned into monsters," said Huggly. "Look!"

The three friends gazed out the bedroom window.
It was dark outside. But they could see weird creatures
rushing from house to house.
"Very strange," said Booter.

They watched a group of the creatures carry
bags up to a house and knock on the door. The
door opened. A people hand reached out and
dropped something into each of their bags. One
creature lifted something off its head.

"Look!" said Booter. "The creatures are just
people children."

"And they're eating snacks!" said Grubble.

"The people in the houses are giving them snacks!"
said Huggly. "Maybe they'll give us some, too."

"We can't go out there," said Grubble. "The people
will catch us."

"Some of those people creatures look a lot like us,"
said Huggly. "Maybe tonight they won't notice that
we're monsters."

The three of them found some paper bags that had been thrown into the wastebasket. Then they followed Huggly downstairs to the front door.

Carefully, Huggly, Booter, and Grubble stepped outside. Suddenly they heard a voice behind them.

"I didn't hear you knock." It was the people mother, and she had caught them! The three monsters froze with fear.

"Those are very nice costumes," she said. Then she added, "Well, aren't you going to say 'trick-or-treat'?"

Huggly had never spoken directly to a people person before. Finally he stammered, "T-t-trick-or-treat?"

The people mother smiled and dropped something in each of their bags. "Happy Halloween!" she said and shut the door.

"Yea-a-ay!" Grubble cheered. "Huggly, you're a genius! Let's get some more goodies."

The three monsters hurried out into the crowds of other creatures. They gathered treats from every house in the neighborhood.

Every house . . . but one.
"I wonder why no people children have gone up there," said Huggly.
"More treats for us!" said Grubble.
"Let's go!"

The dark, old house creaked and groaned when they stepped on the porch. When Grubble knocked, the door swung open with a screech. But no one was there.

"I don't think I like this place," said Huggly.

"There must be treats in here somewhere," Grubble
insisted. He stepped inside.
"Come on," said Booter. "There's nothing to be afraid of."
She followed Grubble.

Huggly didn't want to be left alone on the porch, so he scrambled inside after Booter. The door screeched and then closed—SLAM! Huggly tried to open it again, but he couldn't.

"Booter! Grubble! Come help me!" he said, tugging at the doorknob. No one answered. "Booter? Grubble?"

They were gone!

Huggly searched through the dim, dusty room.
His knees began to tremble. "B-B-Booter?" he
whispered. "G-G-Grubble?"

He stepped around a corner . . .

and faced a monster!

"Yi-i-i-i-i-ikes!" yelled
Huggly. But then he realized
he was seeing himself in a
mirror.

"Whew!" he said. "That
was silly. I scared myself."
He wiped cobwebs from his
head and turned.

"**BOO!**" yelled a ghost.

"E-e-e-e-eek!" Huggly
cried. He spun away and
ran—SMACK—into a wall.

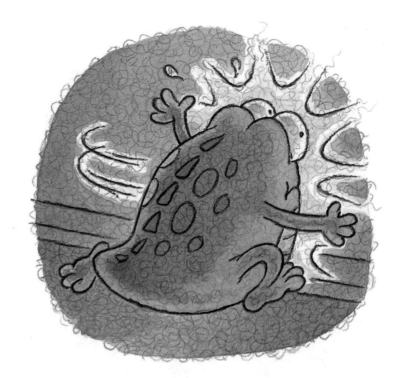

"Ha-ha-ha-ha," the ghost laughed.
Huggly looked up from the floor.
"Grubble?" he asked.

Grubble pulled a white cloth off his head. "Huggly, you looked so scared!" he said, still chuckling.

"That wasn't funny," said Huggly. "Where's Booter?"

"I don't know," said Grubble. "I've been looking for treats."

Together they searched room after room, but they couldn't find Booter. They crept down a very l-o-o-o-o-ng, very dark hallway.

"**BOO!**" said a giant metal monster. CRASH! CLANG!
It stepped in front of them and waved a gleaming sword.

"A-a-a-a-ah!" Grubble and Huggly both screamed and tripped over each other trying to run away.

"Hee-hee-ha-ha-ha!" the metal monster laughed.

Huggly and Grubble looked up from the floor. "Booter?" they asked.

Booter pulled the head off of the metal monster. "You two looked so scared," she said, still chuckling.

"That wasn't funny," said Huggly. "So quit laughing
and help us get out of here!"

"Well," said Booter, "what do we use when we can't
use a door?"

"A bed!" said Huggly.

"Why didn't I think of that?" said Grubble.

The monsters raced upstairs to the first bedroom they saw.

Booter and Grubble dived under the bed. Then Huggly remembered the bag of treats he'd left downstairs. He looked out the bedroom door but decided not to go down into the spooky, old house again. He turned back to the bed.

"**WHO**...?" a little people skeleton
started to speak. It climbed out of bed.

"That isn't funny!"
said Huggly. "You can't
scare me again, Booter.
Or is it Grubble?"

Huggly lifted up the
skeleton's head. It wasn't
Booter or Grubble!

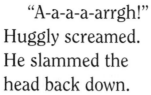

"A-a-a-a-arrgh!"
Huggly screamed.
He slammed the
head back down.

Then he dived under the bed as quickly as possible.

"I heard a scream," said the skeleton father.

"Is everything okay in here?" asked the skeleton mother.

"I . . . I saw . . . a monster from under the bed," the little skeleton whimpered.

"A monster under the bed?" said his mother.
"Tell us all about it."